THE COVER

Yvette Laura-Lawrence

About the Author

I am proud to be the first person in my family to write a book driven by a desire to leave a lasting legacy. As a Gospel Minister deeply in love with the Lord, I am an ardent soul winner who has led many to Jesus Christ. Over the years, I have served and assisted numerous pastors and supported families in need, including those who have lost their homes and the homeless. My passion for helping others is unwavering.

The Holy Spirit inspired me to write my book, "THE COVER," to share my journey and faith. In addition to my ministry, I am a Gospel Singer with a song titled "Lord, I Praise Your Name" and more music set for release.

As an entrepreneur, I founded Dominion & Royalty LLC in 2022. This small business designs T-shirts, bags, hats, flyers, photos, and thermal and spiral books. I am honored to have received the Presidential Award 2024 for my contributions.

I am blessed with a loving family, including my supportive spouse and two wonderful boys. My life is dedicated to serving the Lord and positively impacting the world.

Yvette Laura-Lawrence

Acknowledgments

I want to thank my precious and strong mom, Lula Fleming, for not giving up on me in what I wanted to do. She is my role model. I also want to thank my apostle, David Philemon, for pushing my spirit and way of thinking about my life and purpose. You taught me how to wake up my destiny. Thank you both with gratitude and love

Introduction

Greetings, book reader. I was zealously inspired to write this book by the Holy Spirit called THE COVER. The goal and vision of this book is to encourage readers to take a close Look at life and observe where it has and has brought them. Many times, we, as human beings, find ourselves falling into challenges and various situations that leave us with question marks in our thoughts and minds that want answers. This book will teach you how to win battles. We cover up issues that won't leave until we face them and master them. You are reading the right book, beloved ones. This book will give you answers. I have something to share.

Table of Contents

Chapter 1
Stay Covered Up

Covered by our Heavenly Father, we are protected, clothed, and sealed. It's just like when you are cooking; you put a lid on the pot to protect whatever you are cooking so nothing can hinder your goal of how you want your food to taste. The book of *Psalms 91:1* says, *"He that dwelleth in the secret place of the Most High shall abide under the shadow of the Almighty,"* and verse 4 of this Samuel chapter says, *"He shall cover thee with his feathers, and under his wings shalt thou trust: his truth shall be thy shield and buckler."*

If we keep the Lord's covering over us by dwelling in Him and He in us, seeking His face, believing and receiving what Jesus' word says, and applying it to our everyday lives, we will see more results. Cover also means protection. You may wonder where I'm going with this; when the Lord told me to write, I started writing. I said to myself, "Call it the cover." I thought, "Will I start?" The Lord said, "Just start writing," so I did.

Chapter 2
Don't Be Desperate

The Lord said that this title, "The Cover," also refers to people who always try to cover up things; for example, in *2 Samuel 11:24*, David sinned with Bathsheba, and he had her husband put on the front line. David found out that Bathsheba was pregnant and had her husband killed on purpose, meaning he was placed on the front line so David could cover up his mistakes. I believe this was so David wouldn't feel guilty.

There was another character in the Bible named King Saul, who tried to cover up his sins. The Book of *1 Samuel 15:1-35* talks about how the man of God named Samuel gave Saul instructions on what to do to Amalek in *1Samuel 15:1-3* and in verses 4-35 of 1Samuel explains the rest of the story, how King Saul tried to cover up his sins as he rebelled against God. The Lord used Samuel to tell King Saul to destroy the Amalek and all they have, but King Saul spared King Agag and the best animals.

Chapter 3
Rest, But Pay Close Attention

At times in this life, we go through things that leave us in a horrible state that nobody can fix but God. But do we let God handle it, or do we open up to Satan and allow him to leave us stagnated, depressed, with no understanding, and without faith? The book of *1 Peter 5:7* says, *"Casting all your care upon* him, *for* he *careth for you."* Now remember that the word of God, also reminded us in *I Peter 5:8* says *"*Be *sober, be vigilant; because your adversary the devil, as a roaring* Lion, *walketh about, seeking whom he may devour."*

When a person is not sober, it means that person is not calm and collected or using good sense and judgment. When a person is sober, they will have wisdom and be vigilant. They will be careful and watchful for possible danger or difficulties. They are wide awake, very alert, and watchful. The moment you take your eyes off Jesus Christ, you lose your covering in Him. When someone is brought out into the opening and exposed. *Luke 12:2* says, *"*For *there is nothing covered, that shall not be revealed, neither hid, that shall not be known,"* and verse 3 says, *"Therefore, whatsoever ye have spoken in darkness, shall be heard in the light; and that which ye have spoken in the ear, in closets, shall be proclaimed upon the housetops."*

Chapter 4
Stay Open to God

We need to be covered under the blood of Jesus, the anointing, the fire of God, the shadow of the Almighty, the glory, and the will of God for Jesus' plan and destiny for your life. Sometimes in life, we fall by the wayside, but don't give in to your flaws; they can break you. Don't allow the spirit of fear and condemnation to torment you into a place of stagnation where you feel like you can't get back up and soar again.

Your failures are under the blood. Jesus has placed our sins into the sea of forgetfulness, and He doesn't remember them anymore. But I must remind you to always confess your faults to God when you make an error or operate in that "stinky flesh." In our flesh dwells no good thing, as *Romans 7:18* says. If you read further in the *Samuel* chapter, verses 1-25 talk more about our 'stinky flesh.'

Chapter 5
Do You Know What Happened?

We must continue to watch, pray, and examine ourselves because of the flesh. The words sin and temptation are still in the land, and Satan is behind every episode of it. Satan is our enemy, but remember that we are our own worst enemy. Now, Satan does present temptation to us and makes us curse ourselves. The book of *James 1:14-15* says, *"Every man is tempted when he is drawn away from his own lust and enticed."* Keep reading the book of *Genesis 3:3-14*; when the serpent deceived Eve to eat off the wrong tree, the serpent twisted the word of God in verses 4-5 of *Genesis*.

The Lord had already given the word of God, His instruction, and command to Eve, but she let the serpent deceive and trick her into believing what he said. In verse 6 of *Genesis*, Eve was drawn away by her own lust and enticed Adam, her husband. She gave him the fruit, and he ate it. They were both covered at first by God our Heavenly Father, but when they both ate the fruit of the knowledge of good and evil, they became uncovered.

Chapter 6
Open Secrets

The verb "cover" means to put something, such as a cloth or lid, on top of or in front of something to protect or conceal it. The noun "cover" means a thing that lies on, over, or around something, especially to protect or conceal it. If you look at *Genesis 3:8-24*, Adam and Eve cursed themselves. When Adam heard God's voice walking in the garden, they hid themselves. But honestly, I believe Adam and Eve didn't want God to know they had disobeyed His command. Satan will always give us desire to do things that are contrary to the word of God to keep us bound and yoked up when the word says, *"Whom the son has set free is free indeed."* We should never get to where we are bound by what God gave us the power to bind. In *John 8:36*, we are supposed to live free indeed.

That's why it is very important to stay connected with our Heavenly Father and remain under His covering, where it is safe and secure. We have no power to cover ourselves. In Him, we live, and in Him, we move, and in Him, we have our being. Without Jesus, we can do nothing. *Proverbs 28:13* says, *"he that covereth his sins shall not prosper: but whoso confesseth and forsaketh them shall have mercy."* As *Micah 7:19* says, we have a Savior, our advocate, who will place our sins into the sea of forgetfulness and not remember them anymore.

Chapter 7
Know Who You Are

In the book of *Hebrews 4:16,* we can now go boldly to the throne of grace for anything. Always be truthful and honest with the God of the heavens about everything because He already knows our thoughts from afar *(Psalms 139:2).* In *Romans 8:27,* Jesus is our intercessor; he knows the intensity of the heart and the mind of the spirit. In *Mark 4:22* says, "*For there is nothing hidden, which shall not be manifest, neither was anything kept secret, but that it should come abroad.*"

For whatever is hidden, is meant to be disclosed, and whatever is concealed is meant to be brought to light. In *James 4:14* says, "*Whereas ye know not what shall be on tomorrow. For what is your life? It is even a vapor that appears for a little time and then vanishes.*" Beloved, when we cover up things, we allow darkness to come into our lives and overtake us. The Lord nowhere we all are, naturally and spiritually.

Chapter 8
It's A Way Out

In *Proverbs 15:3* says, *"He sits high and looking down low, beholding the good and the evil."* The more things that are in your life that are covered and hidden will always lead to disaster. We try to protect our pride, envy, strife, anger, bitterness, unforgiveness, hurts, gossip, rejection, guilt, shame, sins, wrong spirit, tale barrier, trimester, trader, drugs, porn, masturbation, sex, alcohol, mental abuse, and more. You name it!

The book of Colossians *1:14* says, *"In whom we have redemption through his blood, even the forgiveness of sins."* Yes, we have and will make mistakes, look like a fool, stumble over things, mess up things, but it's not too late to change things. We came here in sin: all we knew was sin. Jesus is our redeemer *(1 Corinthians 6:20)*. He paid the price of Calvary. He bought us back from the sinful bondage of slavery.

Chapter 9
Stay Ready to Be Used at All Times

The book of *Galatians 3:13* says, *"Christ hath redeemed us from the curse of the law."* Continue reading this whole verse. I remember when I first truly gave my heart to the Lord; I wanted to reach the world, but I wasn't spiritually strong or ready enough. I needed more groaning, making, molding, purging, and digging out from the root of my gut—vacuuming, sterilizing, and cleansing of the soul. I felt soaked, dipped, fried, barbecued, and steamed. Broiled and baked.

Only then was I truly ready to go forth in ministry because there was still a lot of baggage that needed to come out of me so that the demons wouldn't challenge me, saying, *"Jesus I know, Paul I know, but who are you?"*

I would have been just like the Seven Sons of Sceva in the book of *Acts 19:13-16*. The book of *Galatians 5:24-25* says, *"They that are* Christ *have crucified the flesh with the affections and lusts."* Verse 25. In the book of *Romans 8:13*, *"If we live in the* spirit, *let us also walk in the* spirit. *For if* ye *live after the flesh,* ye *shall die, but if* ye *through the spirit* do *mortify the deeds of the body,* ye *shall live."* Let's look at the cover from another perspective in *Jeremiah 3:15*, *"and I will give you pastors according to my heart, which shall feed you with knowledge and understanding."* We are still talking about the cover.

Chapter 10
Know Your Covering

Your pastor is your covering if they are not a hireling. I'll talk about that more later. Every sheep needs a covering to cover them in prayer, in battles that they can't fight spiritually, in sacrifices, on the altar of fire, the anointing, and the power of the highest God of the heavens. You are not on the Samuel level as your covering (pastor or apostle), just like you are not on the Samuel level as your boss.

They call the shots, not you, because of their elevated level—a level you have not reached. They have the ability to hire, and they can fire. If you have children, they are not on the Samuel level as you. You are the boss, and what you say goes. That's why God said He will give us pastors, which is our covering, because our Lord knows the level your covering is on and what they can handle.

Chapter 11
Sacrifice Unlimited

Our pastors and apostles are watchmen and protectors who are strong and courageous with a spiritual backbone. They are never tired; they refire themselves. They are never depressed or stressed out. They don't give up. Our coverings are deep, electrifying fighters, and they don't lose their spiritual light. They have the spirit of a lion. Our covering is always wide awake to pray and intercede for us while we sleep.

They don't quit because they are tired; they quit because they are finished. Have you ever watched a movie called *Rocky*? Who was the boxer playing in this show? He never gave up, no matter how painful it was to win in the ring. Rocky continued to keep moving in his pursuit, and he never looked back. Rocky was severely wounded and bruised, but he continued his race. Muhammad Ali was another boxer who kept refiring.

They cover you from the devil. That's why it's very important to stay connected to your ordained covering, so you can stay covered and protected from all different types of demonic arrows that you can't see coming after you and your family. Book of *Amos 3:7* says, *"Surely the Lord God will do nothing, but he revealeth his secrets unto his servants, the prophets.* Jesus Christ was a coverer to his disciples. Book of *John 17:9-12* says, *"I pray for them, I pray not for the world, but for them which thou hast given me; for they are thine."*

Chapter 12
Don't Be Double Minded

When it's a horrible tornado, the media always warns America to go down in the basements, where there is safety so you can be covered. Do you go outdoors uncovered? The answer is no; you wear garments and shoes on your feet. Beloved, it's very important for you to not let anyone separate you from your spiritual covering, that the Lord has ordained for you. Don't let the serpent talk in your ears and deceive you, especially when you know that they are your true ordained covering.

The book of *Matthew 24:4* says, *"Jesus answered and said unto them, 'Take heed that no man deceives you.'"* The book of *1 John 4:1* says, *"Beloved, believe not every spirit, but try the spirits whether they are of God: because many false prophets are gone out into the world"*. The book of Exodus talks about Moses being the covering for the children of Israel.

Chapter 13
Protected

There is a certain anointing and fire of God that a coverer needs to be in place. For example, a teacher must know how to cover that classroom excellently. This means if a teacher is in charge of a classroom, they should know how to structure the class, letting the boss know they can handle what they have been entrusted with.

Psalms 91:4 says, *"He shall cover thee with* His *feathers, and under* his *wings* shall *thou trust: His truth shall be thy shield and buckler."* God's covering is an expression that describes the spiritual protection and nurture that God provides for all those who are in a covenant relationship with Him. Can you see his cover? The answer is yes, you can certainly experience the effect that it has.

Chapter 14
The Hand of God

I remember, back in the 1990s, when I was scheduled to move out of the apartment, I was living in. The next day, I decided to leave my purse at home on the bed. This purse had a lot of money in it. I took my children to school, and when I returned, I noticed the mirror in the washroom had been pulled out of the wall. I could visually see the other apartment's bathroom, and that's when I knew something was wrong.

My apartment had been broken into, and then I remembered I had left my purse with money on the bed. Beloved, this is not a wise choice; please don't consider it. I needed this money to vacate the apartment and move to another neighborhood. So, I went back into my bedroom and saw my purse. I looked inside to see if the money was still there. Oh my God, this is a praise break right now. Yes, the money was still there, in Samuel's place. Now listen to this: the robber went into Samuel's room where my purse was, took several other items, but didn't touch the purse. The book of *1 Corinthians 1:9* says, *"God is faithful, by whom ye were called unto the fellowship of his Son Jesus Christ our Lord."*

Chapter 15
Have Discernment

The Lord is faithful to His promises. I thanked God. The Lord will cover and protect everything we have. Why do we cover up our sins when that's all we know—sin? *Romans 7:23 says, "But I see another law in my members, warring against the law of my mind, and bringing me into captivity to the law of sin which is in my members."*

Evil was always present when I would do good, trying to get me to yield to temptation. That's why we must constantly ask the Lord to purge us with hyssop from all ungodliness, unrighteousness, and unholiness; back to my story. I started going back to places from my past, trying to witness to old friends and even visit an old boyfriend to witness to him too. But the Lord showed up just in time to warn me that now I am in the light, and I can't keep going back to the dark. I was just a babe in Christ, desiring the sincere milk of the word.

I wasn't strong enough yet. I saw an open vision while I was standing there. The vision showed me that the place I kept visiting was dark. I witnessed the earth turn pitch black, even though it was daytime. Then I heard God say to me, *"If you continue to follow Jesus' path, you will see the Samuel light that Jesus showed me illuminate the earth."*

Fearful, I decided to distance myself from my old company. Satan had a hidden trap set for me, and the Lord loves me so much that He wanted me to see it. It was up to me whether I would adhere to or obey Him. The choice was

15

mine. I chose life. I was not filled with the Holy Ghost; I didn't have any power to overcome the devil *(Acts 1:8)*. I wasn't fully covered.

Chapter 16
Stay on Fire

We need power in electricity for certain things to function or operate. Power for lights to turn on, power for a TV to function, and power for an engine in a car to operate. Some of these things I mentioned are all protected by a certain covering to make them work and function properly. If something is not connected correctly or aligned, these objects will not function.

In the book of *Acts 1:8*, it says, *"But ye shall receive power after that the Holy Ghost is come upon you; and ye shall be witnesses unto me."* Finish reading this whole verse. Now, back to what I was saying earlier about Acts 19:15-16: if I hadn't obeyed the Lord's voice or vision, an evil spirit would have leaped on me, overcome me, and prevailed against me.

Remember, I was completely uncovered, and Satan knew that. That is why it's very important to be led by the Spirit of God and not by yourself, because a lot of times, we lean on our own understanding.

Proverbs 3:5 says, *"trust in the Lord with all thine heart and lean not unto thine own understanding."* Because a lot of times, we make so many mistakes, and stumble when we lean to our own understanding. Understanding means the ability to understand something, to comprehend, to perceive the intended meaning of things. To interpret or view something in a particular way. Also, read verses 6 and 7 of Proverbs.

Chapter 17
Don't Assume Victory

Don't be so full of yourself that you can't accept correction. Satan tells you not to go to church anymore, and then you start saying, *"I'm anointed, power-packed, and ready for action. Watch my smoke!"* Don't misunderstand me—when a believer is filled with the Holy Ghost, there are still things inside that need to be flushed out, things that are not like God.

Even so, you will still have power over all the powers of the devil. To remind you again, we are on Satan's hit list. He is a roaring lion who walks about, seeking whom he may devour. We must constantly pray without ceasing and work out our own salvation with fear and trembling. Also, put on the whole armor of God so that you may be able to stand against the wiles of the devil. There are different types of coverings that we need.

Chapter 18
Stay Connected

Genesis 3:1 talks about how Satan is very subtle; he has a lot of patience, and Satan watches and watches closely and checks on our progress when we become saved and born again. The book of *Luke 11:24-25* clearly explains what I am trying to say, when you receive deliverance from anything or are free from past habits, you must not look back or become weak because those Samuel spirits and habits will come back seven times worse. In *Matthew 12:43-45*, it talks about what happens to a person when they lose their covering. *1 Peter 4:8* speaks of a covering; love is the greatest of them all.

Isaiah 5:1 talks about the covering that God placed over Israel, but they didn't acknowledge what Jesus was doing. The Lord gives us everything we need to survive in this world. It's our responsibility to take heed of what He has done and to guard it. God gave Israel every covering to prevent Satan from sabotaging their inner growth. The Lord was specially working on them so they could be used for His glory.

Israel didn't take this purging seriously, and that's why their inner man was made of wild grapes and not grapes. In *Isaiah 5:4*, the cover is more than what you think. If a car doesn't have a top on it while you're driving, rain and snow can cover you. You want that protection versus someone who has a covering on their car. Humans need clothes to cover their flesh. When it rains, you use an umbrella. When it snows, you wear a hat, gloves, boots, a scarf, and a winter coat for protection from feeling cold. In *Exodus 28:42*, it says, "*And thou shall make them linen breeches, to cover their nakedness; from the loins even unto the things they shall reach.*" I remember when I was in grade school (Catholic Grade School), I always wanted to wear my mom's outfits, but she told me not to. I was tempted by my own lust and desires. I waited until she went to work, then went into my mom's closet, grabbed my favorite outfit that belonged to my mom, and wore it to school. I did this more than once.

I thought I was getting away with it, but one day, when it was time for gym class, I had to change into my gym uniform. I went into the bathroom to change but forgot to put my mom's outfit in my book bag. I left it in the bathroom. I went to the gym to play, but when the gym period was over, I realized the outfit I had secretly worn had been stolen from the bathroom.

Oh Lord, I knew that my seat behind me was going to be very heated from the discipline that was coming to me at home. I stopped wearing the covering of obedience and yielded to the covering of disobedience, where there was no safety at all. I was guilty as charged. The principal had to call my mom and let her know that I didn't have a change of clothes to put on.

That's when everything I was trying to cover up was revealed. I was scared and embarrassed because my mom would finally know what I had been doing behind closed doors.

The book of *Luke 12:2* says, *"There is nothing covered, that shall not be revealed; neither hid, that shall not be known."* We need to be covered under the blood of Jesus, the anointing, and the fire of God. The shadow of the Almighty God, the glory, and the will of God. Jesus has plans and a destiny for your life.

Chapter 19
Negative Pardons

Hebrews 13:17 says, *"Obey them that have the rule over you and submit yourselves: for they watch for your souls."* 'Submit' means to accept or yield to a superior force or to the authority or will of another person. It means to cease fighting or arguing, to yield, and to surrender. Submit also means to allow room for someone or something else. *In James 4:6-7*, it says that God resists the proud and gives grace to the humble. 'Proud' means having self-respect or improper and excessive self-esteem, known as conceit or arrogance."

Proud people may do good work; however, it's usually for the sake of their own praise. Also, the book of *1 Peter 5:6* says, *"Humble yourself therefore under the mighty hand of God, that he may exalt you in due time,"* you know, in our flesh dwelleth no good thing. Humble means to be respectful, lower in dignity, or important. Quiet, gentle, and easily imposed on; submissive.

What did Paul say in *Romans 7:14-25, "For we know that the law is spiritual: but I am carnal, sold under sin. For that which I do I allow not: for what I would, that do I not; but what I hate, that do I."* Read the other verses in this Samuel chapter. Beloveds, if you keep believing it's your way or no way, we will wind up like Samuelson in the Bible. Look at *Judges 16:16-21.* Samuelson thought that he was still covered and had it down-packed.

He thought that his power, anointing, and strength couldn't be stripped from him. But, brothers and sisters, when you become full of yourself, puffed up, proud, and think you have it all sealed together, Satan will attack your weaknesses and present them to you openly, just as he did to Samuelson.

Look at verses 19 and 20; don't yield to pride, temptation, or rebellion, or you will lose your hair, your anointing, and strength to fight off things that are constantly monitoring your every move. These are called monitoring spirits. In the book of *Matthew 26:41,* it says, *"Watch and pray, that* you *enter not into temptation: the spirit indeed is willing, but the flesh is weak."* Temptation means the desire to do something, especially something wrong or unwise; it also means a thing or course of action that attracts or tempts someone. A strong desire or impulse. David was a man after God's own heart. In *Psalms 51:4*, it says, *"Against thee, thee only have I sinned, and done this evil in thy sight,"* when David had Bathsheba's husband Uriah put on the front line to be killed.

David acknowledged what he had done and humbled himself according to the law. We must observe to do according to examine ourselves; *Ephesians 5:15* says, "See *then that ye walk circumspectly, not as fools but wise, Redeeming the time, because the days are evil."*

Chapter 20
Observe and Examine

Also, read verses 17 in the book *Revelations 2: 1-29* and *Revelations 3:1-22*; there were seven churches and among the seven churches. Some issues needed to be addressed. The Lord was not pleased with some of the churches, but he was pleased with some of the churches.

God is concerned about how we live our everyday lives. Are we concerned? Do we notice anything unusual in our lives that is not spiritually functioning properly? Man and King have been created and shaped in his image, which needs immediate attention right away with no hesitation.

Conclusion

I hope that this book has been inspiring and encouraging to my world. I want you, the reader, to take a moment and think and meditate about your life, value and time, and what really makes sense to human nature. We are to be special role models to our world, for example, our families and friends. Be encouraged, very strong, and know that you can make it. Let the Lord take your hand and lead and show you the way to a safe path.

www.ingramcontent.com/pod-product-compliance
Lightning Source LLC
Chambersburg PA
CBHW041031170626
46815CB00001B/56